WISH

A story by Ian Bragg

Copyright

About the author

Ian Bragg serves as Vice President of Research and Statistics in the investment management industry. A lifelong writer of fiction and poetry, his debut published story showcases his deep connection to the natural world and passion for adventure.

It was the first day of summer and Alistair awoke when the sun reached inside his window and shone its warm golden light on his face. He put the kettle on to make tea for himself and for his Mom and Dad who were still asleep in the room next to the kitchen. As he did most summer mornings, Alistair took his tea and sat outside on the front steps of his small wooden house, and looked down into the mountain valley. He enjoyed these quiet moments when he was alone and there was little farmwork to be done. Today, the valley was exploding in colour with the purple and pink from thistle and heather. He watched the cattle his family owned quietly grazing in the fields below.

As he was drinking his tea, he watched a small white seed tuft of a flower rise up from the valley, drift over his head, and then blow high up into the air. As he continued to follow it, the tuft finally disappeared into the bright blue sky above. He quietly made a wish and whispered it into the gentle breeze.

The summer was filled with these seed tufts. His mother had told him that if you make a wish on one of them and it reaches the sky, the wish will be granted. From then on, he called these tufts wishes.

Alistair wondered to himself if wishes really do come true when they reach the sky. He thought, quite practically, that many of the small white wishes would get caught on the ground and wouldn't make it to the sky. But what about the ones that do make it? He wondered how he could really know. How could he prove it one way or the other?

Suddenly he had an idea.

"I'll make a test," he said to himself. "I'll bring a wish high up the mountain behind my home and when I'm there, I'll make a wish on it and blow it up into the sky."
If what he was told was right, his wish would come true.

As his parents slept, Alistair packed water, an apple, and two cookies in a backpack. He also took an empty jar from the kitchen and carried it in his hands. He walked quickly to the trail that led to the mountain peak.

It seemed to Alistair that this was the beginning of the most important adventure of his life. He was going to prove to the world if wishes really do come true.

But Alistair needed one very important thing first. And he found it. Just to the side of the mountain trail, he plucked a small white seed tuft that was caught on a purple thistle. He carefully placed it in the jar and put the jar in the side pocket of his backpack.

Alistair started to hike up the mountain trail. He thought about what people wished for. He thought about some of the wishes that he had made. All morning he hiked and when the sun was high in the sky he got to a small open grassy area where he had picnicked with his Mom and Dad the previous summer.

He opened his pack and ate his apple and cookies. He was only going to have one cookie and save the other for the way down but he was too hungry and he couldn't resist. As he was sitting, a hawk rose up from the valley below him and flew right by his head. Alistair could hear the wind in the hawk's wings and see its bright orange eyes. How lucky the hawk is, Alistair thought. He can fly wherever he wants.

After drinking some water, Alistair was back on the trail. While the hiking seemed easy in the morning, the trail became more difficult and started to narrow and get steeper. Instead of a soft mountain trail, he started climbing over jagged rocks. He knew that his Mom and Dad would not approve of this part of his journey and he began to wish that he wasn't alone.

Alistair continued to climb. Higher and higher. Further than he had ever gone before. The air seemed thinner and it was getting harder to breathe. It was also getting wet. He was now as high as the clouds and was actually inside the clouds. Occasionally a cloud would cover him in cold damp air. Alistair thought it was interesting that when you are inside a cloud, it doesn't look white and fluffy. It looks grey and misty. He wished that he had brought his thick wool sweater. He thought about turning back but he was so high now he thought that he must be close to the top.

Alistair had been hiking and climbing for what seemed like hours. He sat down on a rock to rest and to drink more water. He was so cold that he began to shake and he wrapped his arms around his legs in an effort to keep warm.

He watched ants scurrying about his feet, carrying bits of things back to a hole in the ground. He was comforted by the fact that he wasn't completely alone. He soon realized that stopping was a bad idea. Without moving, he was getting even colder. He knew that if he didn't reach the top soon he would have to turn back. He grabbed his bag and jumped up and continued up the mountain.

Just as Alistair was about to give up, there he was…he had reached the top! The sky had cleared and he could see all the way down the mountain valley. It was the most spectacular view he had ever seen. He was so high that he could not even see his house or the cows or anything else that he recognized down below. He felt as though he was on top of the world. Higher than even the hawk flies!

As excited as Alistair was, he was also nervous. The sun was starting to go down and his body was casting a long shadow on the ground. Realizing that he didn't have much time, he bent down to get the jar from the side pocket of his pack. It was gone! He opened his bag and dug his hand around the inside but couldn't find it there either. He pulled the bag wide open. Nothing! It must have fallen out when he stopped for a snack, he thought. He couldn't believe it! "Was this whole hike up the mountain for nothing," he said to himself. He felt like crying.

Just as Alistair was about to head back down the mountain, his eye caught a patch of grass in the distance. In the grass were thousands of little wishes. It was so dense with wishes that it looked like a white cotton sheet was placed on the grass. It was beautiful and shining as the orange light of the setting sun glowed like fire on the wish-covered grass.

Were these wishes blown by children from all over the world that had become trapped, he wondered. He thought that maybe, just maybe, all these wishes would come true if he lifted them up into the sky.

Alistair knew that he was running out of daylight and that he risked having to climb down in the dark if he took any more time on the top of the mountain. But he couldn't leave knowing that he might be able to help thousands of childrens' wishes come true. With that thought, he ran through the field with his hands raking the grass, freeing the wishes and throwing handfuls into the air. As Alistair ran, he looked up and saw the wishes, thousands of them disappearing into the darkening sky.

When Alistair had finished freeing the wishes, he started to climb back down the mountain. It was slow going. He was cold and there was very little light. Each step had to be carefully considered. After what seemed like two hours of climbing, he lost his focus and made a bad step. A loose rock gave way under his foot and Alistair slid off the trail and tumbled down against a boulder. He had bruised his knees and his hand was bleeding. A cold wind was now whistling in his ears. He didn't know where the trail was anymore. He felt like he just could no longer go on.

As he started to cry, he could see through his blurry eyes that there was a single wish, caught in a plant right by his nose. He carefully put it between his trembling fingers. He closed his eyes and he made a wish. He blew it into the cold air that was rushing around him and it was carried high into the air. After that, Alistair drifted off.

"Alistair!" "Alistair!" Yelled his Dad.

The yelling woke Alistair up.

"I'm here Dad. I'm here!"

The next thing Alistair knew, his father was carrying him in his arms down the mountain.

When Alistair was back in his bed with his hand bandaged and thick wool blankets tucked tight against him, he told his father and mother about his trip. He told them about the field of wishes and how he knew that all the wishes came true.

His father asked him: "Alistair, how do you know that the wishes came true"?

Alistair said, "I know, because you came for me. Just as I wished!"

THE END

Manufactured by Amazon.ca
Bolton, ON